Football Superstar
Aaron Rodgers

by Jon M. Fishman

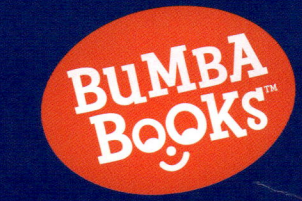

LERNER PUBLICATIONS • MINNEAPOLIS

Note to Educators

Throughout this book, you'll find critical-thinking questions. These can be used to engage young readers in thinking critically about the topic and in using the text and photos to do so.

Copyright © 2020 by Lerner Publishing Group, Inc.

All rights reserved. International copyright secured. No part of this book may be reproduced, stored in a retrieval system, or transmitted in any form or by any means—electronic, mechanical, photocopying, recording, or otherwise—without the prior written permission of Lerner Publishing Group, Inc., except for the inclusion of brief quotations in an acknowledged review.

Lerner Publications Company
A division of Lerner Publishing Group, Inc.
241 First Avenue North
Minneapolis, MN 55401 USA

For reading levels and more information, look up this title at www.lernerbooks.com.

Main body text set in Helvetica Textbook Com Roman 23/49.
Typeface provided by Linotype AG.

Library of Congress Cataloging-in-Publication Data

Names: Fishman, Jon M., author.
Title: Football superstar Aaron Rodgers / by Jon M. Fishman.
Description: Minneapolis : Lerner Publications, [2019] | Series: Bumba books—sports superstars | Includes bibliographical references and index. | Audience: Age 4–7. | Audience: K to Grade 3.
Identifiers: LCCN 2018038339 (print) | LCCN 2018040227 (ebook) | ISBN 9781541556522 (eb pdf) | ISBN 9781541555624 (lb : alk. paper)
Subjects: LCSH: Rogers, Aaron, 1983– —Juvenile literature. | Quarterbacks (Football)—United States—Biography—Juvenile literature. | Football players—United States—Biography—Juvenile literature.
Classification: LCC GV939.R6235 (ebook) | LCC GV939.R6235 F575 2019 (print) | DDC 796.332092 [B]—dc23

LC record available at https://lccn.loc.gov/2018038339

Manufactured in the United States of America
1-46017-42934-10/10/2018

Table of Contents

Leader of the Pack 4

Football Gear 22

Picture Glossary 23

Read More 24

Index 24

Leader of the Pack

Aaron Rodgers is a superstar quarterback.

He throws passes for the Green Bay Packers.

Aaron grew up in California.

He loved to watch the

San Francisco 49ers on TV.

Football was Aaron's favorite sport.

He played football in high school.

He also played soccer, basketball, and baseball.

Why do people play different sports?

Aaron went to college.

He played quarterback there.

In 2005, Aaron joined the

Green Bay Packers.

Brett Favre was Green Bay's top quarterback.

Aaron watched Brett to learn more about playing quarterback.

How do other people help us learn new things?

Brett left Green Bay. In 2008, Aaron became the team's top quarterback.

Aaron played like a superstar. He helped Green Bay win the Super Bowl in 2011.

Aaron helps make his team great. He wants to win the Super Bowl again!

Football Gear

Picture Glossary

college — school after high school

passes — throws in a football game

quarterback — a football player who throws passes

Super Bowl — the championship game in pro football

Read More

Flynn, Brendan. *Football Time!* Minneapolis: Lerner Publications, 2017.

Nelson, Robin. *From Leather to Football.* Minneapolis: Lerner Publications, 2015.

Osborne, M. K. *Superstars of the Green Bay Packers.* Mankato, MN: Amicus, 2019.

Index

college, 10

Green Bay Packers, 4, 13–14, 17–18

high school, 9

quarterback, 4, 10, 14, 17

Super Bowl, 18, 20

Photo Credits

Image credits: Amy Salveson/Independent Picture Service (football icons throughout); Andy Lyons/Getty Images, pp. 5, 23 (top right): David Madison/Getty Images, pp. 6–7; Seth Poppel Yearbook Library, p. 8; Robert B. Stanton/WireImage/Getty Images, pp. 11, 23 (top left); AP Photo/Julie Jacobson, p. 12; AP Photo/Morry Gash, p. 15; AP Photo/David Stluka, p. 16; David Eulitt/Kansas City Star/MCT/Getty Images, pp. 19, 23 (bottom right); Larry Radloff/Icon Sportswire/Getty Images, pp. 20–21; Mtsaride/Shutterstock.com, p. 22 (football); Mathew Hayward/Alamy Stock Photo, p. 22 (helmet); Elvert Barnes/Flickr (CC BY-SA 2.0), p. 22 (jersey); Roman Samokhin/Shutterstock.com, p. 22 (cleats); Joe Robbins/Getty Images, p. 23 (bottom left).

Cover: Todd Kirkland/Icon Sportswire/Getty Images.